STERLING CHILDREN'S BOOKS
New York

An Imprint of Sterling Publishing
387 Park Avenue South
New York, NY 10016

Library of Congress Cataloging-in-Publication Data Available
Distributed in Canada by Sterling Publishing
c/o Canadian Manda Group, 165 Dufferin Street
Toronto, Ontario, Canada M6K 3H6
Distributed in the United Kingdom by GMC Distribution Services
Castle Place, 166 High Street, Lewes, East Sussex, England BN7 1XU
Distributed in Australia by Capricorn Link (Australia) Pty. Ltd.
P.O. Box 704, Windsor, NSW 2756, Australia

For information about custom editions, special sales, and premium and corporate
purchases, please contact Sterling Special Sales at 800-805-5489
or specialsales@sterlingpublishing.com.

Printed in China
Lot #:
2 4 6 8 10 9 7 5 3 1
03/12

www.sterlingpublishing.com/kids

SILVER PENNY STORIES

Jack and the Beanstalk

Told by Diane Namm
Illustrated by Maurizio Quarello

There was once a brave boy named Jack. He and his mother lived in a small cottage. They were very poor. The only valuable thing they owned was a cow named Milky-White.

The day came when Milky-White no longer gave them milk.

"Take her to market," Jack's mother said. "Be sure to get a good price!"

Feeling sad, Jack led Milky-White away.

Soon Jack grew tired. He sat by the roadside. Along came an old man.

"I'll buy your cow and pay with these," he said.

The old man opened his hand.

"Beans!" Jack scoffed.

"Magic beans," the old man said. "Plant them, and overnight you'll have the finest bean plants in all the world. They are better than money or an old cow!"

Jack took the beans, handed over the cow, and went home to his mother.

"How could you sell the cow for beans?" his mother moaned. "What will we live on?"

Jack's mother flung the beans out the window and sent Jack to bed without supper.

The next morning when Jack awoke, there was a strange green light in his room.

Jack looked out the window. There he saw a huge beanstalk that reached up to the sky.

"Those beans must be magic!" he said.

Jack dressed and quickly climbed up the beanstalk. Higher and higher he climbed until he reached the top. He found a road and followed it until he came to a great palace. There he smelled a delicious smell.

When Jack reached the palace door, a woman opened it.

"Goodness! My husband will eat you for breakfast!" she exclaimed.

She hid Jack in the oven. Then they heard a frightening sound.

"Fee, fi, fo, fum. I smell the blood of an Englishman. Be he alive or be he dead, I'll grind his bones to make my bread," boomed the giant's voice.

"There's nothing here but your bacon and eggs," said the giant's wife.

The giant wolfed the food down in two great bites. Then he pulled out a large sack from his pocket.

The giant poured out a pile of gold coins. He began to count. Before long, he fell fast asleep at the table.

Jack crept out of the oven.

Jack grabbed the sack and the coins from the table and ran out of the giant's kitchen. He climbed down the beanstalk and rushed home.

"Mother, we're no longer poor!" said Jack.

He told his mother what had happened.

They used the money to buy food for many days. But one day the money ran out. So Jack climbed back up the beanstalk.

This time, the giant's wife wasn't friendly.

"Aren't you the boy who was here the day our gold was taken?" she asked.

"Oh, no," Jack said.

Just then they heard a frightening sound.

"Fee, fi, fo, fum. I smell the blood of an Englishman. Be he alive or be he dead, I'll grind his bones to make my bread," boomed the giant's voice.

Jack jumped into the oven.

"Silly, man. There's no one here but us," she told the giant.

Grumbling, the giant brought out a beautiful hen.

"Lay an egg, hen," he commanded.

The hen laid a solid gold egg!

Jack popped out of the oven, grabbed the hen, and ran out of the palace.

"ARRRRRGH," the giant roared and chased after Jack.

Jack slid down the beanstalk with the giant close behind. Using an axe, Jack chopped down the beanstalk. *SNAP!* With a mighty crash, it split the ground. The giant tumbled down, down, down.

The giant was never seen or heard from again. Jack, his mother, and the beautiful hen lived happily ever after.